BOOK CLUB EDITION

Library of Congress Cataloging in Publication Data: Main entry under title: Walt
Disney Productions presents Tod and Copper from The Fox and the Hound. (Disney's
wonderful world of reading ; 49) SUMMARY: A young fox and a puppy form a
friendship, but as they grow up, they realize that their relationship cannot stay the
same. 1. Foxes—Legends and stories. 2. Dogs—Legends and stories. [1. Foxes—Fiction.
2. Dogs—Fiction] I. Walt Disney Productions. II. Title: Tod and Copper. III. Series.
PZ10.3.F8354 [E] 81-2619 AACR2
ISBN: 0-394-84819-5 (trade); 0-394-94819-X (lib. bdg.)
Manufactured in the United States of America

R S T U

0 1 2 3

WALT DISNEY PRODUCTIONS

presents

TOD and COPPER

FROM *The Fox and
the Hound*

Random House  New York

One spring morning, Big Mama the owl
sat watching the world.

She saw a mother fox run out of
the woods.

The fox raced across the field.

Near the fence she dropped something
in the grass.

Then the fox ran
back into the woods.

Suddenly Big Mama heard
a gunshot.

The mother fox did not return.

"Oh, dear!" said Big Mama.
"Maybe a hunter killed that
poor fox."

Big Mama wanted to see
what the fox had dropped.
    She flew down to the fence.
There was a baby fox!
    "Oh, my!" said Big Mama.
"We will have to find
a home for you!"

Big Mama called her friends over to see the fox.
"I think we need Mrs. Tweed's help," she said.
Mrs. Tweed owned a farm nearby.
Right now she was in the barn, milking a cow.

Mrs. Tweed heard a lot of noise outside.
She ran out to see what was the matter.
Some birds were making a fuss by the fence.
"I'm coming," called Mrs. Tweed.

Mrs. Tweed found the baby fox.
She took it home with her.
She named the little fox Tod.
Mrs. Tweed took good care of him.

Every day Tod played with the farm animals.

One day Tod followed a butterfly . . .

. . . right into the woods.

In the woods Tod found an old cabin.

The cabin belonged to a hunter named
Amos Slade.

Amos had an old dog named Chief and
a new hound pup named Copper.

Chief was a hunting dog.

Copper was going to be a hunting dog, too.

Chief was
a fine hunter—
when he was
awake!

Copper had a good sense
of smell.
Today he smelled something
different.

Copper went to see what
the new smell was.

His nose led him straight to
a hollow log.

At the end of the log he saw
Tod, the little fox.

"What are you doing?" asked Tod.

"Tracking something!" said Copper.

"What are you tracking?" Tod asked.
"I think it's you!" said Copper.
The little fox began to laugh.
The puppy laughed, too.
By the time they finished laughing,
Tod and Copper were friends.

Tod and Copper played together every day.
They did not know that foxes and hounds
were not supposed to be friends.

Amos Slade did not know
who Copper played with.

But one day he tied Copper up.
"I don't want you running
around," Amos told the puppy.
"Good hunting dogs stay put!"

Tod came to see his friend.
"I can't play with you anymore,"
said Copper. "I have to stay here."

"Who is that big dog?" asked Tod.
"Be careful!" said Copper. "That
is Chief. Don't wake him up!"

But Chief was already
awake.

He opened one eye and
saw the little fox.

The old dog growled.

Tod was scared!

He raced off as fast as
he could.

Tod ran into the henhouse.
The hens were afraid of him.
They jumped up and squawked!

SQUAWK! SQUAWK! SQUAWK!

Tod got out of the henhouse—fast!

Amos Slade heard the hens squawking.
He came out of his cabin and saw the fox.

"Stay away from my chickens!" yelled Amos.
"If I see you again, you'll be sorry!"

Summer ended and fall came.

It was time for Amos to teach Copper
how to hunt.

"We are going on a long hunting trip,"
Amos told Copper and Chief.

He loaded up his truck.

The dogs were both excited.

Copper sat in the back of the truck.
He saw his friend Tod by the road.
And Tod saw his friend Copper going away.
Both Tod and Copper felt sad.
They would miss each other.

A lonely Tod went to see Big Mama.

"When Copper comes back next spring," she said, "he won't be your friend anymore."

"That is not true!" said Tod. "Copper and I will always be friends."

All winter Amos taught Copper to be
a hunting dog, just like Chief.

At first it was hard work.

But by the end of winter, Copper
knew how to hunt.

Copper was even
smarter and faster
than Chief.
"Now I have two
good hunting dogs,"
Amos said proudly.

Amos, Chief, and Copper
came home in the spring.
Copper felt very important.
He was a big dog now—with
a big job.

A few days later, Tod came to visit.
Chief was sleeping, as usual.

"Hi, Copper," said Tod. "You have really grown."

"Yes, Tod," said Copper. "So have you."

Chief was having an exciting dream.
It was a dream about foxes.
In the dream Chief heard some voices.
Slowly he opened one eye.
And there was a real fox!

Tod and Copper did not know that Chief was
waking up.

"Are we still friends?" asked Tod.

"We can't be friends anymore," said Copper.
"I am a hunting dog now."

All at once Chief leaped at Tod!
The big dog growled and barked.

"Run, Tod! Run!" Copper shouted.

Amos Slade dashed out of his cabin.
"There is that fox again!" he cried.
"This time he won't get away!"

Amos quickly untied the dogs.
They both started chasing the fox.
Tod knew he was in terrible danger.
He ran for his life!

Through the woods . . .
across the fields . . .
up a cliff . . .
Tod ran and ran.
He looked behind him.
The dogs were still
following!

Finally Tod was too tired to run anymore.
He hid under a stack of boards.
It was a good hiding place.
Chief went right by.

But Copper had a good nose.
He came along, sniffing the ground.
His nose led him straight to Tod.
Tod was trapped.
He had no place to go.

Copper heard Amos
climbing up the cliff.

"I don't want you to be
killed, Tod," said Copper.
"I will let you go."

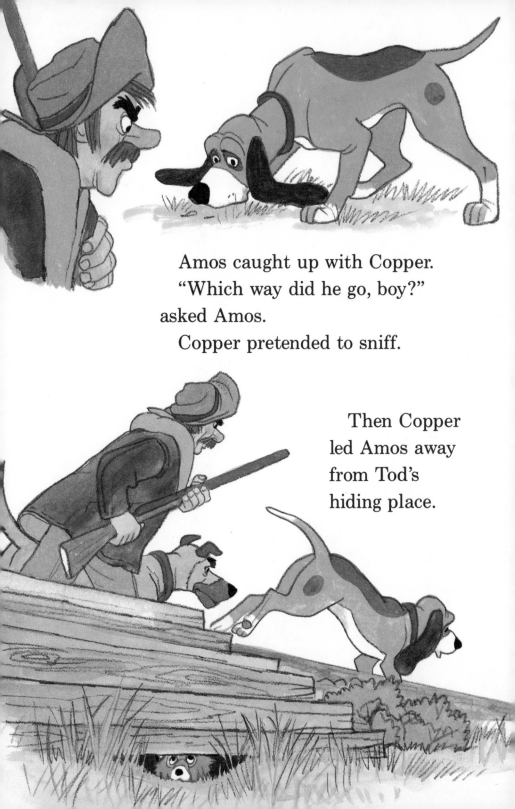

Amos caught up with Copper.
"Which way did he go, boy?"
asked Amos.
    Copper pretended to sniff.

Then Copper
led Amos away
from Tod's
hiding place.

Soon Amos and the dogs were gone.
Tod crawled out of his hole and
ran for home.

Now he knew what hunting dogs did.
They hunted foxes!

Tod found Mrs. Tweed at the fence.
"Someone has been chasing you!" she said.

She hugged
the fox.
"I'm glad
you are safe,"
she told him.

That night Tod thought about his friend Copper.
And Copper thought about his friend Tod.

They both knew that they could never play
together again.

But Tod knew that he loved Copper.

And Copper knew that he loved Tod.

THAT would never change.